That's Not

By Gerry Kruger

ISBN: 9798448509872

Published by The Creative Short Book Writers Project
Wayne Drumheller, Editor & Founder
Printing Platform: KDP.Amazon.com
Cover Design and Illustrations

That's Not Fair is published and copyrighted in 2022 as a First Edition. It is published by The Creative Short Book Writers Project, Wayne Drumheller, Editor and Founder. Final editing and editorial assistance is by Gerry Kruger. Photographs, illustrations and notes are ® registered by the author and editors. The quotes and notes found in this book are, to the best of their abilities, what they felt, believed and remembered when they were spoken, read or inferred to them. Special acknowledgements have been granted for use of quotes and images that appear in this book from public and private sources. No part of this book may be reproduced or transmitted in any form or by any means, electronic or mechanical, including photocopying, recording or by any information storage and retrieval system without permission from the author and editors, except for brief quotations embodied in news articles or otherwise specified.

League of Women Voters of the Charlottesville Area

The League of Women Voters encourages informed and active participation in government, works to increase understanding of major public policy issues, and influences public policy through education and advocacy.

The League of Women Voters never supports or opposes candidates for office, or political parties, and any use of the League of Women Voters name in campaign advertising or literature has not been authorized by the League.

Our local League has taken action on several issues that concern our community. Committees meet regularly, communicate with legislators, write letters, attend rallies, hand out flyers, and present programs designed to educate the public. Currently we are most active on issues related to gun violence prevention, affordable housing, election integrity, health promotion, child care, combating climate change, and public schools.

Contents

Introduction, p. 3
Content---That's Not Fair Coloring/Activities. p. 4-37
Acknowledgements, Resources and References, p. 38
About The Author, p. 39
Activities, p. 40-45

ABOUT THE LEAGUE
MISSION STATEMENT

The League of Women Voters encourages informed and active participation in government, works to increase understanding of major public policy issues, and influences public policy through education and advocacy.

We do not endorse or oppose candidates for political office, or political parties.

We are committed to applying the principles of diversity, equity, and inclusion in all of our operations and activities.

We support governmental policies that apply these principles in addressing the social, environmental and economic problems in our communities.

We hold governmental officials accountable for decision-making that promotes widespread, informed and civil public participation.

Maud Wood Park (1871-1955)

Maud Wood Park campaigned for suffrage and women's rights at colleges throughout the United States. In 1901, she was one of the founders of the Boston Equal Suffrage Association for Good Government that became the League of Women Voters in 1920.

INTRODUCTION

The League of Women Voters of the Charlottesville Area hopes this book will show young readers the importance of voting and the role the League plays in supporting voting in our democracy. We hope to promote reading among young people and provide books that engage as well as inform future voters.

The story introduces the reader to two nine-year-old girls from different backgrounds, who become friends on the swings in a park. The mother and grandmother of Rochelle are members of the League of Women Voters, and the mother of Christie wasn't allowed to vote in a prior election. Since the League promotes diversity, equity, and inclusion as an essential part of their program, this story emphasizes black history in keeping with this idea.

Thanks to her mom and grandmother, Rochelle discovers how the suffragists long ago fought for voting to be fair and open to all people. She also sees the League at work encouraging and preparing citizens to vote.

On a warm September day, nine-year-old Rochelle Davis and her mother Leona walked five blocks to the park. A few puffy white clouds were scattered in the bright blue sky above the leafy green trees that surrounded the park.

Leona pointed to a tall maple tree. "Rochelle, come to the League of Women Voters table by that tree if you need anything. We'll be registering voters until six o'clock." She paused to face her daughter. "Be careful on the swings."

"I will, Mom." Rochelle watched her mother stroll toward a table where two ladies and a man were spreading out brochures and voter registration papers.

Dashing to the swings, she could hardly wait to feel the gentle breeze brush through her shiny black braids as she soared into the air.
She sat down in the first of three swings and began to pump her legs. Feeling free and loose made up for sitting in a desk most of the day at school.

Soon a girl with a blonde ponytail sat in the swing next to her. She was wearing light blue shorts and a white tee and looked about Rochelle's age.

Rochelle smiled and shouted from her swing, "Hi, I'm Rochelle. What's your name?"

"I'm Christie." She watched Rochelle swing higher and higher. "Do you live around here?"

"We live five blocks down that way." Rochelle stopped swinging and pointed in the direction of her house. "How about you?"

Christie pointed to the apartments across the street and began to swing. "My mom and I live there. I come here almost every day while my mom's at work."

"Lucky you. My mom doesn't let me come by myself."

"You're by yourself today, aren't you?"

"No, my mom's with the people by that tree. Christie looked around and spotted the women and the man. "Oh, what are they doing?"

"They're registering voters for the election in November. Is your mom registered to vote?"

"I don't know. She tried to vote one time and they wouldn't let her."

"THAT'S NOT FAIR! My mom says everyone should be able to vote."

"That's what I say, but my mom has two jobs. Even if she is registered to vote, she doesn't have time to vote in between."

Rochelle shook her head. "THAT'S NOT FAIR EITHER! Is your mom at work now?"

"Yeah. I wish she didn't have to work so much. What about your mom? Does she work?"

"She's a teacher and my dad's a computer analyst."

"You're the lucky one. You probably get to see your parents a lot."

"I guess you're right. My mother and grandmother belong to the League of Women Voters. I'll talk to them tonight about helping your mom to register to vote."

LEAGUE OF WOMEN VOTERS

"I've heard of that. Is there a League of Men Voters too?"

Rochelle thought for a second. "I don't think so. Some men belong to my mom's league though. My dad's a member. That man at the registration table probably is too."

Christie looked around and smiled. "Yeah, I see him"

"I'll tell my mother about your mom tonight."

"Thanks, Rochelle. Will you be here tomorrow to tell me what she said?"

"Maybe. My mom may let me come by myself if you're gonna be here."

That afternoon Rochelle told her mother about meeting Christie in the park. "She lives in the apartments across from it. Her mom can't vote because she has two jobs and doesn't have time to vote. I told Christie it wasn't fair."

Mrs. Davis rested her forefinger on her chin. "Tell Christie your father and I would like to visit and register her mother to vote. Then we can try to answer any questions she has about voting."

"Perfect!" Rochelle gave her mother a high five. "Does that mean I can go to the park tomorrow and meet her?"

"Maybe. Promise me you won't talk to strangers, and come home if there's nobody else around."

"Yes, ma'am!"

THAT'S NOT FAIR

Rochelle and her mother were cleaning up after dinner when Mrs. Davis stopped and asked her daughter, "Did you know there was a time when women couldn't vote?"

"THAT'S NOT FAIR!" Rochelle declared. "Why was that?"

"After the Civil War, the 15th Amendment was passed." It said the right to vote couldn't be denied on account of race.

Mrs. Davis added, "Black or white, women couldn't vote."

Rochelle stomped her foot. "NOT FAIR!"

Her mother continued, "Both white and black women from all over the country started fighting for women's suffrage. Suffrage means the right to vote. One of the best known was Susan B. Anthony. Anthony was once arrested for trying to vote."

"NOT FAIR!"

Mrs. Davis smiled. "And Carrie Chapman Catt was the founder of the League of Women Voters. She trained under Susan B. Anthony and continued to fight for women's suffrage."

"Were those women black or white?"

"Susan B. Anthony and Carrie Chapman Catt were white, but some of our black sisters also fought hard."

"Elizabeth Piper Ensley was an African-American suffragist and professor at Howard University in Washington D.C. She moved from there to Boston and then to Colorado, where she joined the National Association of Colored Women (NACW)."

President Woodrow Wilson

Rochelle liked learning about women who stood up for themselves. Her mom told her they were called suffragists because they were fighting for women's suffrage.

Mrs. Davis looked at Rochelle to be sure she was still listening.

"At first the President at the time, Woodrow Wilson, didn't support Women's Suffrage. He changed his mind because of the demands from women. In 1920 he signed The 19th Amendment. It gave women the right to vote."

Elizabeth Piper Ensley

1847-1919

"Could all women vote in 1920?"

Rochelle noticed her mother's watery eyes. Mrs. Davis took a deep breath and spoke softly.

"Even though the 15th Amendment and the 19th Amendment had been passed, it wasn't until the 1960's that most black voters could exercise their right to vote. But in Colorado, where Elizabeth Ensley moved, women won the right to vote in 1893.

"Elizabeth Ensley started the Colored Women's Republic to show women of color how to vote and why they should vote. She also pushed for a national women's suffrage amendment. She wanted all women in the United States to be able to vote."

Leona Davis rubbed Rochelle's shoulders. "Grammy's coming over tonight. She can tell you how all black women got the right to vote."

Later, when Grammy rang the doorbell and stepped inside, Rochelle ran into her open arms. Grammy gave her a tight squeeze. "How's my favorite granddaughter?"

Rochelle grinned. "Mama said you could tell me how black women got suffrage."

"Well, aren't you a smart one! Tell me what suffrage is."

Rochelle stood tall and answered. "It means the right to vote. How did black women get the right to vote?"

Rochelle loved Grammy's visits. The two sat on the living room sofa and shared another big hug. Rochelle couldn't wait to hear about the fight for black women's suffrage.

Grammy sank back into the yellow pillows on the sofa and began. "After white women won the right to vote, there were many people who didn't want us to vote. During the 1960's Blacks in the South began to demand their rights. They held marches, sat in restaurants that had 'Whites Only' signs, and marched in the streets."

Rochelle shook her head. "The 1960's came forty years after the 19th Amendment! It took them a long time to get started."

In Memory of and Dedication to Maggie Lena Walker:
America's First Black Female Bank President

1864-1934

Maggie Lena Walker was the daughter of a freed slave and an Irish-born Confederate soldier. She rose from poverty to become an entrepreneur, civic leader, and the first African American woman in the United States to charter a bank and serve as a bank president. After the 19th Amendment was passed, she helped organize voter registration drives and voter education events. Her rise to prominence during difficult times for many women, especially African American women, was extraordinary.

Grammy smiled at her granddaughter's math skills. "Those 40 years were hard for black folks. Some people tried to keep us from getting our rights by doing horrible things. The Ku Klux Klan burned a cross in my grandmother's yard. Some of my relatives were killed for trying to register voters."

Rochelle felt hot tears trickle down her face. This was more than not fair. It was a crime. "And the police didn't make them stop doing those things?"

"Most were never arrested. A few who went to trial were found not guilty. Finally, we decided enough was enough! Black people began to fight back. Marie Foster was one of them. One Sunday in 1965, six-hundred marchers planned to walk 54 miles from Selma to Montgomery, Alabama. When they got to the Edmund Pettus Bridge, lawmen attacked them with clubs and tear gas. The beating that Marie Foster received was caught on film. People around the country saw the injustice our people suffered."

Marie Foster   Eleanor Holmes Norton

"Grammy, is Marie Foster still alive?"

"No, she died in 2003. But another woman who was a civil rights leader is still alive and fighting for our rights today."

"Who is she?"

"Eleanor Holmes Norton. In the 1960's she was a college student and an organizer for the Student Nonviolent Coordinating Committee, known as SNCC. She registered African American citizens to vote in Mississippi in 1964. Now, she represents the District of Columbia in Congress."

"Miss Eleanor has been fighting for our rights, for a long time, Grammy."

"Yes, child."

"What was the first year black women could vote?"

President Lyndon Johnson signs the Voting Rights Act with Martin Luther King, Jr. and other civil rights leaders in attendance. National Archives (NARA)

"In 1965 President Lyndon Johnson signed the Voting Rights Act, which made it possible for thousands of blacks to vote for the very first time. All the people I've told you about are heroes, black and white. They fought for something larger than themselves. They fought for our democracy. Your vote is your voice. America will be stronger if all our voices can be heard."

Grammy leaned back and put both hands on her granddaughter's shoulders. "If you must fight for something that isn't fair, fight for something larger than yourself."

"Yes, Grammy, I will, thanks to you."

Christie Wheeler had headed home after Rochelle left the park. She was anxious to tell her mom about the League of Women Voters. When her mother finally walked in, Christie was finishing a peanut butter and jelly sandwich.

"Mom, I met a girl at the park today. Her mom is in the League of Women Voters and wants to help you register to vote in the November election."

Sandra Wheeler smiled at her daughter. "Really? That's nice, but I'll probably just wait until the next presidential election. That's more important."

Christie pleaded, "Oh, Mom. Please let them register you to vote. Rochelle and her mom are so nice. They think everyone should vote."

"I'll talk to my boss. Maybe she'll let me off early if I have something important to do."

The next day, Rochelle could hardly wait for school to end. Her mother had agreed to let her walk to the park to meet Christie, and she was helping someone to vote just as the famous suffragists did. Soon she spotted Christie swinging.

Christie's blue eyes sparkled when Rochelle said her parents wanted to come to their apartment and register her mother to vote. They would try to answer any questions she had about voting.

"Thanks, Rochelle. I hope you come too. I'll ask Mom if I can bake some cookies for us."

The next evening, Leona and Phil Davis met Sandra Wheeler and registered her to vote. The girls went to Christie's room with a plate of chocolate chip cookies.

Leona told Sandra, "We'll help you apply for a mail-in ballot."

"But I'm not sure who's running and who to vote for. I only want to vote for the president."

Leona said, "As an LWV member, I've learned how I can you get the information you need to vote. That's one of the things the League does."

"Many laws are made at the local and state level. That's why local and state elections are important to you. Changing voting laws to make it easier to vote would allow you to vote for candidates that share your concerns.

"And one thing we know is it's important to vote in all elections. Local leaders make decisions that affect you the most. It's the state lawmakers that set the rules for elections. They decide who is allowed to vote by absentee ballot. That would make it easier for you to vote."

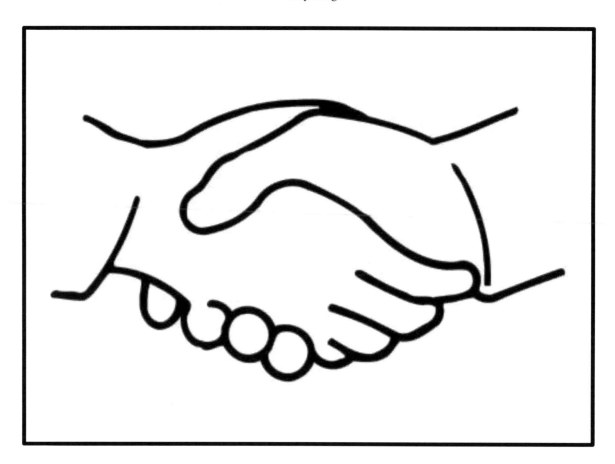

Sandra Wheeler looked pleased. "It's been a pleasure to meet you."

Leona took Sandra's hand.

"The League of Women Voters won't be happy until everyone votes. Our leaders should make laws that are good for all people—rich and poor, all races, all nationalities, and all neighborhoods. This can happen only if every citizen goes to the ballot box in every election."

The next day the park was abuzz with children soaring on swings, scooting down the sliding board, and hurling frisbees.

But only two children in the park were suffragists. They wanted what was right and just for all people. They were walking and talking side by side.

Acknowledgements

The League of Women Voters of the Charlottesville Area appreciates the efforts and support of these members and friends who helped write and edit this book:

Beth Alley, Beth Kariel, Carol Cutler, Carolyn Fitzpatrick, Diane Inman, Maggie Hoover, Lois Sandy, Meg Heubeck, Pat Cochran, Sue Lewis, Rosalie Simari, Kerin Yates, Eunice Doles, and Michele Kellermann

References and Resources

"Valiant Women of the Vote," *Women's History*, I (March 20, 1921), 12-14.

"Women and the Vote: Centennial Calendar," WNDC Educational Foundation (2019).

Colvard, Bernice. *Virginia Women and the Vote: The Equal Suffrage League and The League of Women Voters in Virginia.* League of Women Voters of Virginia Education Fund, 2009.

"A Glimpse at Virginia's Organized Woman Suffrage Movement: Part II". May 9, 2022 https://rvalibrary.org/shelf-respect/law-library/a-glimpse-at-virginias-organized-woman-suffrage-movement-part-ii/

"Maggie Lena Walker (1864-1934)" https://encyclopediavirginia.org/entries/walker-May 9, 2022 maggie-lena-1864-1934/

 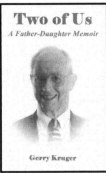 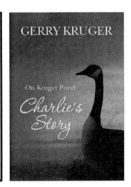

About the Author, Illustrator & Publisher

Gerry Kruger, a native Virginian, moved from Richmond to Charlottesville, Virginia in 1979 where she taught high school English for 27 years. After retiring, she joined the League of Women Voters and studied issues related to public education. Meanwhile, she published two books about Charlie, a lame goose that arrived on foot at her pond. He was also the subject of essays she read on National Public Radio.

Shortly after her father died at the age of 98, she published *TWO OF US: A Father-Daughter Memoir*. Gerry and her father believed people could overcome setbacks and obstacles just as Charlie did with a little help and attention from caring individuals. And, just as the early suffragists overcame barriers to women's rights, today the League of Women Voters still fights to overcome barriers to voting. Gerry received her Bachelor's Degree from Longwood College and her Master of Education from the University of Virginia. (gerrykruger@embarqmail.com)

Mary M. Archer of Mebane, NC is a talented artist, writer and fine arts photographer who has attracted a broader historical audience in the Piedmont of North Carolina region through her partnerships with authors and her latest book, *Fun With Textiles*. It is a creative and interactive teaching tool, she produced with her daughter, Jennifer, to enable children to learn about the textile industry's history and heritage in Alamance County, NC. She was honored to assist Gerry Kruger in illustrating *That's Not Fair*.

Wayne Drumheller, a native of the Rockfish River Valley, Virginia, is the Editor and Founder of The Creative Short Book Writers Project. Since 2010, he has helped over 200 regional writers and artisans publish their narrative biographies, historical memoirs, and collections of prose/poetry/photography/art and nonfiction and fiction books. He received his Bachelor's Degree from California State University at Sonoma and his Master of Education from the University of North Carolina at Greensboro. He is a member of the Virginia Blue Ridge Writers Club and Founder of the Rockfish River Valley Writers and Writer in Residence for the Old Winter Green-Rockfish Valley Rural Historic District.

Activity Pages

NOTE: Permission is granted by the author to photocopy these activity items for educational purposes.

Activities # 1 Match number answer to empty blanks

1. Leona and grandmother
2. In 1965 President Lyndon Johnson
3. Eleanor Holmes Norton
4. Marie Foster
5. Elizabeth Ensley
6. President Woodrow Wilson
7. Carrie Chapman Catt
8. Maggie Lena Walker
9. After the Civil War
10. Maude Wood Parker

___ signed the 19th Amendment In 1920. It gave women the right to vote.

___ signed the Voting Rights Act.

___ registered African American citizens to vote in 1964.

___ was the founder of the League of Women Voters.

___ founded the Boston Equal Suffrage Association which became the League of Women Voters in 1920.

___ the 15th Amendment was passed.

___ started the Colored Women's Republic to show women of color how to vote and why they should vote.

___ on Sunday, March 7, 1965, was scheduled to walk from Selma to Montgomery, the Alabama state capital.

___ belonged to the League of Women Voters.

___ was the first Black bank president in the United States.

Activity # 2. How many words can you make from League of Women Voters

_____ _____ _____

_____ _____ _____

_____ _____ _____

_____ _____ _____

_____ _____ _____

Activity # 3. WORD SCRAMBLE

1. enwom _____

2. fsufrage _____

3. utelas _____

4. ldedep _____

5. giaallegce _____

6. ilohyad _____

7. bserove _____

8. mbsyol_____

9. srats_____

10. pesstri_____

Activity # 4 Maze

Activity # 5

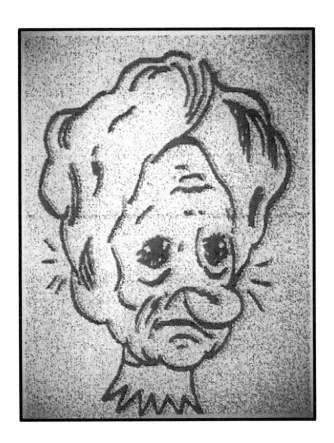

Find the 'young' Princess in the Queen Mother's face.

Activity # 6

Can you make 10 words or more from these signs?

_____ _____ _____

_____ _____ _____

_____ _____ _____

_____ _____ _____

1. Match Numbers to empty blanks: 6, 2, 3, 7, 10, 9, 5, 4, 1, 8

2. LWV: Men, golf, age, gang, mentor, war, lower, goat, lent, fee, feet, foot, loot, eagle, wagon, tower, run otter, gun, water, vote, now, not, later, sea…

3. Word Scramble: women, suffrage, salute, pledge, allegiance, holiday, observe, symbol, stars, stripes… There are many more possibilities:

4. Maze

5. Turn the book upside down

6. Voters, Voting, regulate, Nation, Latino, Uses, Equal, seasons, sun, son, notion, late, let, Letter, Alter, alternate, lesson. The possibilities are endless.

Made in the USA
Middletown, DE
13 September 2022